For Jen, Kate, Shona
and Ella

Written, illustrated, and designed by Carol M. Kearns

Edited by Nicola Sedgwick

ISBN: 978-0-244-18387-5

Marcy Pam

Daisy

Ella

Marcy Pam

A Doll, a Girl and a Fairy

Carol M. Kearns

Part One

Marcy Pam

Once upon a time,
in a tasty cupcake store,
a tiny princess dreamt each day
of jumping to the floor.

There, she would somersault,
dance, skip and hop.
There, she would pirouette,
and never want to stop.

But little princess Marcy Pam
could only wish and dream,
as she sat upon a cake
topped with Marzipan and cream.

For Marcy Pam was plastic,
just a tiny painted doll.
And dolls don't run or jump,
not ever ... not at all!

Ella

Part Two

Ella is a little girl
who also loves to dance.
To music from a jewellery box,
her Aunty sent from France.

But one day,
while happily dancing,
she swung her arms around,
and knocked the box right over,
where it crashed onto
the ground.

"Oh No!" said Ella to her Mom.
"Tell me what to do?
I don't think I can fix this doll
with sticky tape or glue!"

"You dont need my help,"
smiled her Mom.
"I know you'll find a way
to replace that doll
by yourself,
it may even be today!
"But how about, for now?
We both go out to tea.
To Carly's fancy cake store,
a treat for you and me."

So off they went together,
one summer's day in June,
Ella and her Mother,
for a girlie afternoon.

Now, Carly's store is famous,
people come from far and wide,
to taste a cake or two, or three,
from the vast array inside.

It was Ella's first time ever,
to visit the famous store.
And never had she seen
so many cakes on sale before.

There were cream cakes, fruit cakes, chocolate muffins too.
Many shades of birthday cake, from vibrant pink to blue.
Yummy cupcake pictures decorated every wall,
so many cakes to choose from, and Ella liked them all.

But the one that really caught her eye,
and stood out from all the rest,
was the tiny Princess Marcy cake,
which she liked the very best.

So that's the one
that Ella chose,
a choice that was to be,

a lucky thing for Marcy,
and a lucky thing indeed!

Well, Ella and her mother
spent a lovely afternoon,
enjoying time together
in the cupcake store in June.

By the time she got home
she had thought of a plan,
and up to her bedroom
the little girl ran.

She fixed Marcy to the place
where the ballerina used to be.

Clickity-click.
Clickity-click.

She turned the winding key.

Suddenly little Marcy Pam
began to move and twirl,
making Ella jump for joy–
she *was* a happy girl!

And each day
after school,
Ella danced with
sheer delight.

Then under her pillow
she tucked Marcy Pam
each night.

Part Three

Daisy

Daisy is a fairy who has yet to cast a spell.

A spell which will not end up wrong; a spell that turns out well!

And one night,
when Ella's tooth fell out,
the Queen said to the King.
"Send Daisy to collect the
tooth. Let her fairy
work begin."

But the King,
he was a tad
concerned
about sending
her along.

"Don't worry!" said the Queen.
"What could possibly go wrong?

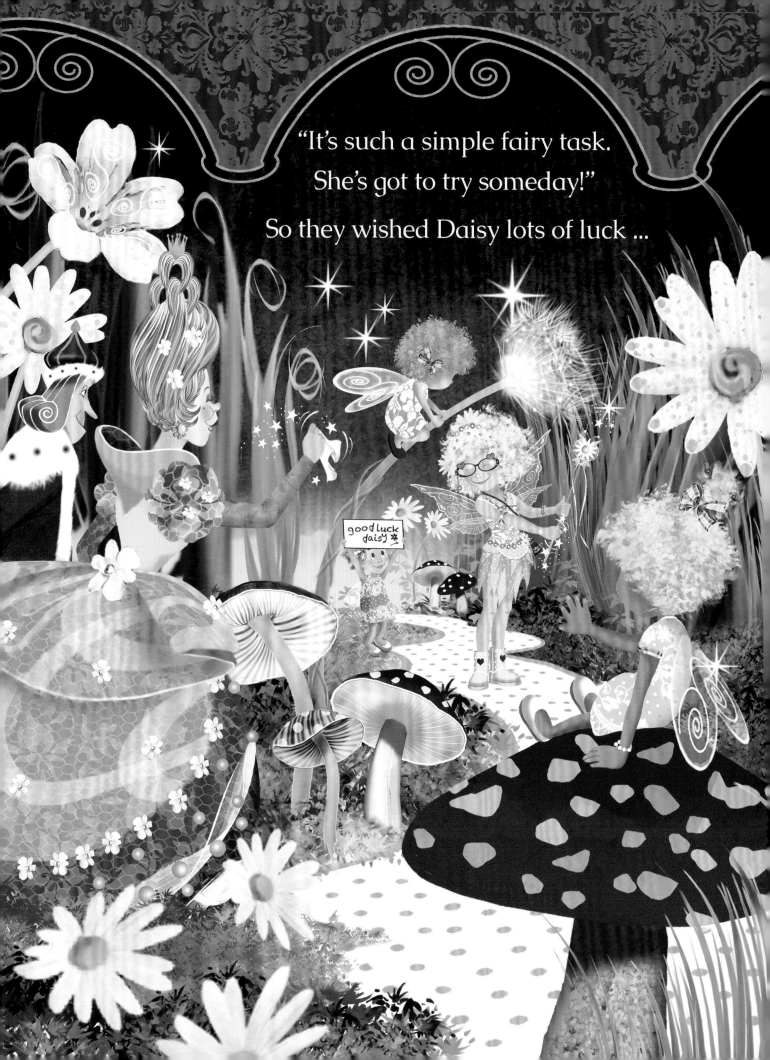

"It's such a simple fairy task.
She's got to try someday!"

So they wished Daisy lots of luck ...

... and sent her on her way.

But at Ella's house, poor Daisy;
things did not start that well.

She clean forgot every word
of the famous toothy spell.

So the little fairy made them up
from deep inside her head.

"La la la!" and
"Loopy dee doo!"

Were the words
she used instead.

As she spoke
she crossed her fingers,
and waved her wand about ...

...Whoosh!

A coin appeared
under Ella's pillow,
and Ella's tooth flew out.

Now, Daisy was so very pleased,
and proud of her toothy spell.

Her first big job collecting teeth
had gone extremely well.

All of a sudden Marcy Pam
appeared out of the blue,
crawling on her hands and knees,
alive like me and you!

Oops!

Daisy's topsy-turvy magic, had turned the plastic doll, into a real-life human girl, although still very small.

"What happened?
Who are you?"
Princess Marcy said.

As the tiny
white tiara,
went and slid
down off
her head.

"My name is Daisy. I'm a fairy.
And I guess that I'm quite clever!
Because I think I am the first tooth fairy,
to create a person — *EVER*"

Ella

"You really are!" said Marcy.
"Look what your magic's done for me!
I'm moving, and I'm twirling—
without winding up a key!"

She somersaulted to the floor
from way up on Ella's bed.

The little fairy
took her hand.
"Let's dance! Marcy,"
she said.

Now, every day
on the jewellery box
Marcy twirled
around,
pretending she was
still a doll,
and never made
a sound.

But every night in secret,
as quiet as a mouse,
she danced and played with Daisy
all around the house.

So Marcy's dream
really did come true.
She even made new friends.

And although there's lots more to the tale, ...

... for now, the story ends!

Marcy Pam is the second picture book written and illustrated by Irish artist Carol M. Kearns. Her first picture book, the delightful Christmas story, *I've an idea!* was published, November 2018. Carol's work has appeared in advertising campaigns, on thousands of greeting cards and in numerous Children's Educational books. Greeting cards and products relating to her picture books are available from her online stores, WilBi Designs on Greeting Card Universe, and WilBi Creations on Zazzle.
Carol lives in Co. Dublin, Ireland.

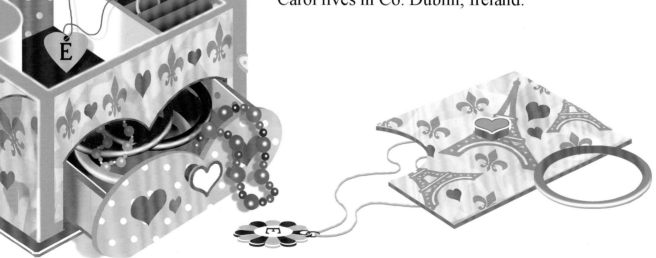